USBORNE FIRST LEARNING

STARTING TO ADD

Karen Bryant-Mole and Jenny Tyler

Designed and illustrated by Graham Round

S0-EGS-685

About this book

This book is for an adult and child to use together and is designed for children who are confident in their use of numbers up to 10. It introduces the concept of addition in a well-structured progression and ensures that the child has all the necessary pre-addition skills such as understanding the order of numbers, working with sets and understanding the concept of 'more'. Toward the end of the book the addition and equals symbols are introduced and their use is reinforced in a progressively more abstract way over the final pages.

The book also includes an addition game that can be used over and over again.

Notes for parents

The first pages of this book are designed to ensure that your child understands basic number concepts, such as individual number recognition and the order of numbers. These are, however, intended to reinforce such concepts and not to act as an introduction to them. If your child is not yet confident with numbers it is recommended that two other books in this series, *Starting to Count* and *Counting up to 10*, are worked through first.

It is best to use this book when both you and your child are in the right mood to enjoy it. Try not to do too much at any one time. If the child seems unready or unwilling to tackle any of the activities, just leave it and come back to it later.

Writing numbers

Many of the pages require the child to write numbers in boxes. Don't worry if your child cannot write numbers well. When she has worked out what the number should be, you could write that number faintly in the box and allow her to write over it. It is important to remember that just because a child cannot write numbers it does not mean that she cannot understand them. Similarly, do not assume that because your child can write a 5 beautifully she has an automatic understanding of that number.

Before you start make sure that your child is holding the pen or pencil correctly. It is easy to develop bad writing habits with the wrong grip.

Pens and pencils should be held lightly between the thumb and first two fingers, about 1in from the point.

More

This seems such a simple word yet it can cause confusion. Children generally hear and use the word in situations such as "Can I have *more* juice please?", i.e. an additional quantity of something. Here, though, you are asking your child to use the word in the context of making a comparison between two sets of objects. You can give your child further practice by collecting two unequal sets of objects, and matching the two groups either by placing them in pairs or by joining them with drinking straws.

It is very important that your child understands the order of numbers and whether numbers are greater (more) or less than other numbers before you begin adding numbers together.

Language

There are no hard and fast rules regarding the language you use to introduce addition. An effective way is to begin by using words that your child understands such as "3 teddies *and* 4 teddies *makes* 7 teddies altogether". When you feel that he understands the task required you can start to introduce other words, such as "add" and, possibly, "equals". Do this by asking the same question in different ways so that your child learns that the phrases mean the same thing. If your child already attends school or you know which school he will be going to you might like to find out which phrases he will use in class and introduce him to these.

Follow-up activities

Many of the pages in this book can be extended with practical activities based on the ideas given. Look, too, for examples of addition in your child's life and help him discover that math is all around us.

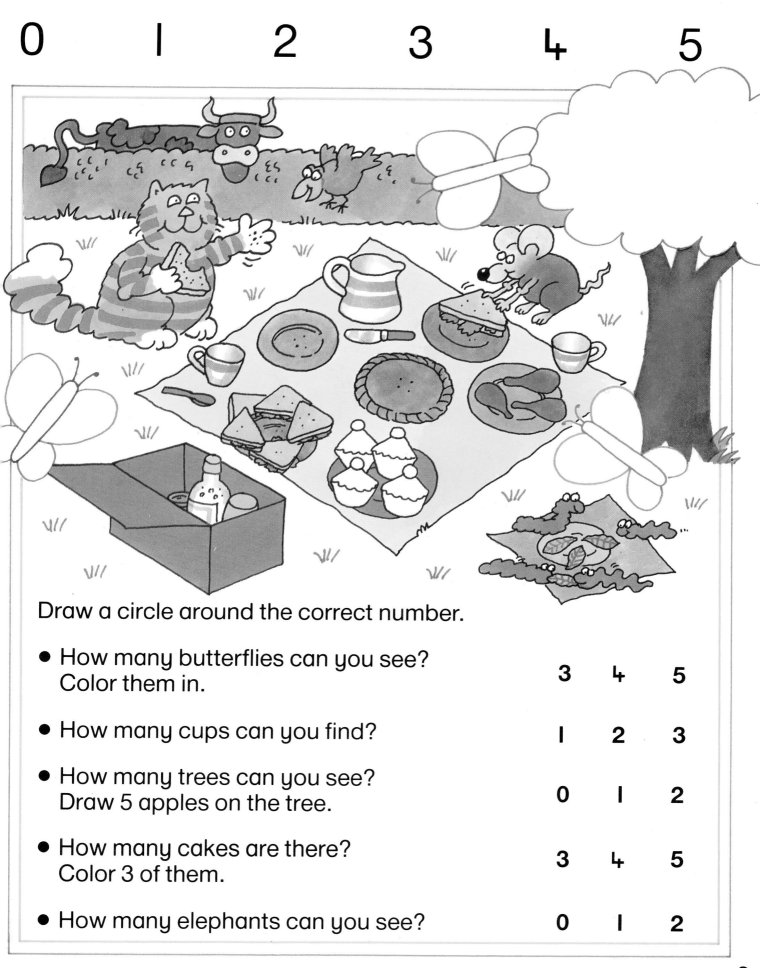

Draw a circle around the correct number.

- How many butterflies can you see?
  Color them in.   3   4   5

- How many cups can you find?   1   2   3

- How many trees can you see?
  Draw 5 apples on the tree.   0   1   2

- How many cakes are there?
  Color 3 of them.   3   4   5

- How many elephants can you see?   0   1   2

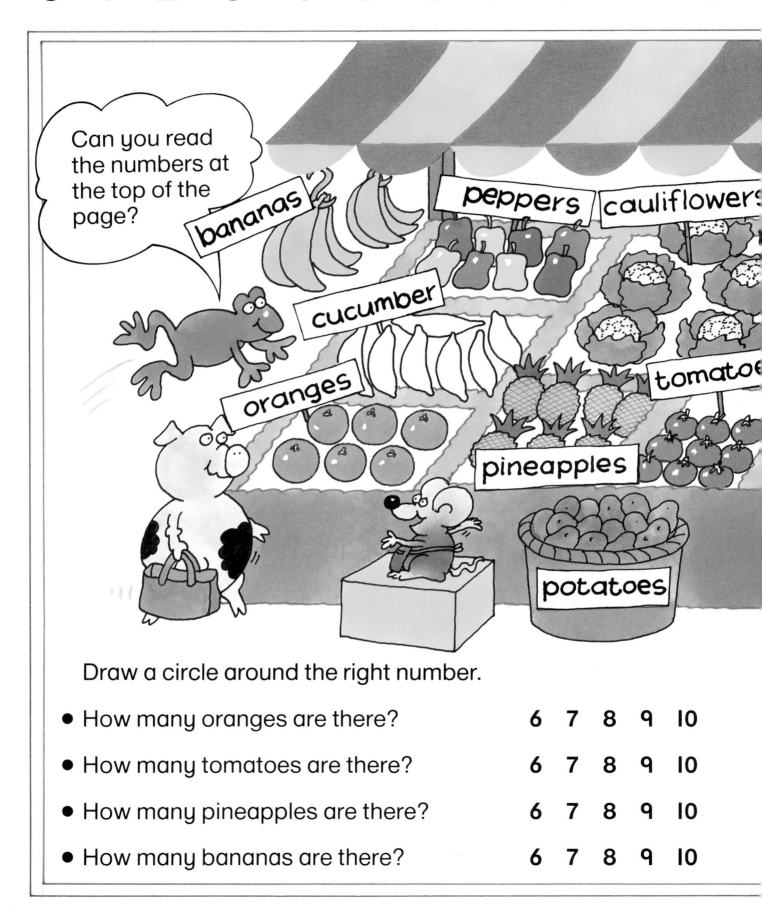

Can you read the numbers at the top of the page?

bananas

peppers cauliflowers

cucumber

oranges

tomatoes

pineapples

potatoes

Draw a circle around the right number.

- How many oranges are there?   6   7   8   9   10
- How many tomatoes are there?   6   7   8   9   10
- How many pineapples are there?   6   7   8   9   10
- How many bananas are there?   6   7   8   9   10

- Color 3 cucumbers.

- Can you find 10 carrots to color?

- How many pears are there?   6 7 8 9 10

- There is something on the stall that doesn't belong there.
  Can you find it and color it?

- How many horses are there?
  Color 1 brown and 1 gray.

- How many sheep are in the field?

- How many pigs
  can you see?

- How many tractors are there?
  Finish coloring it.

- How many
  have spots?

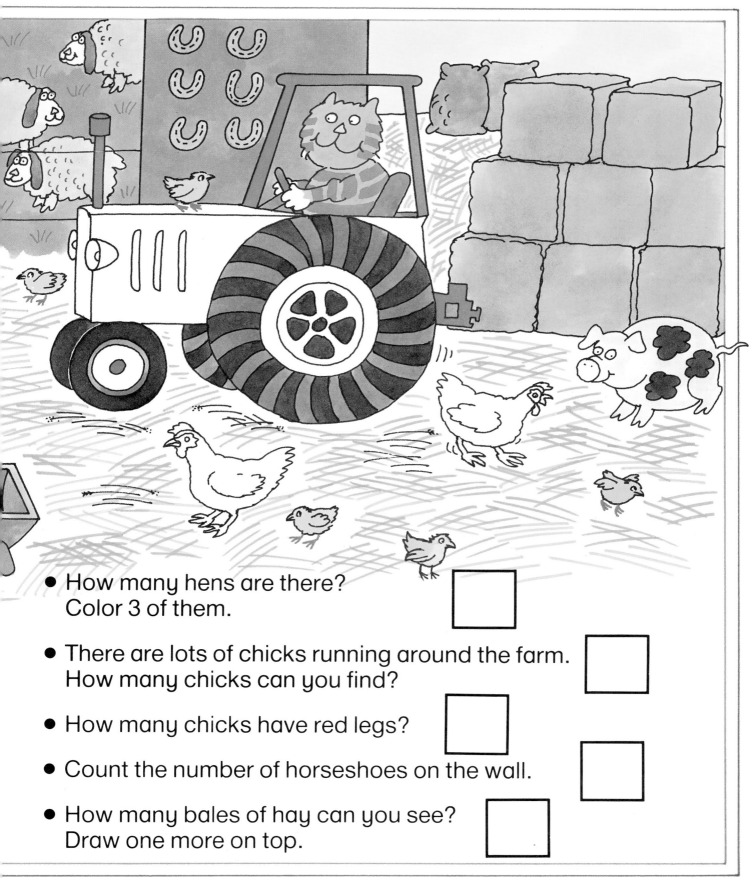

- How many hens are there?
  Color 3 of them.

- There are lots of chicks running around the farm.
  How many chicks can you find?

- How many chicks have red legs?

- Count the number of horseshoes on the wall.

- How many bales of hay can you see?
  Draw one more on top.

Pig painters

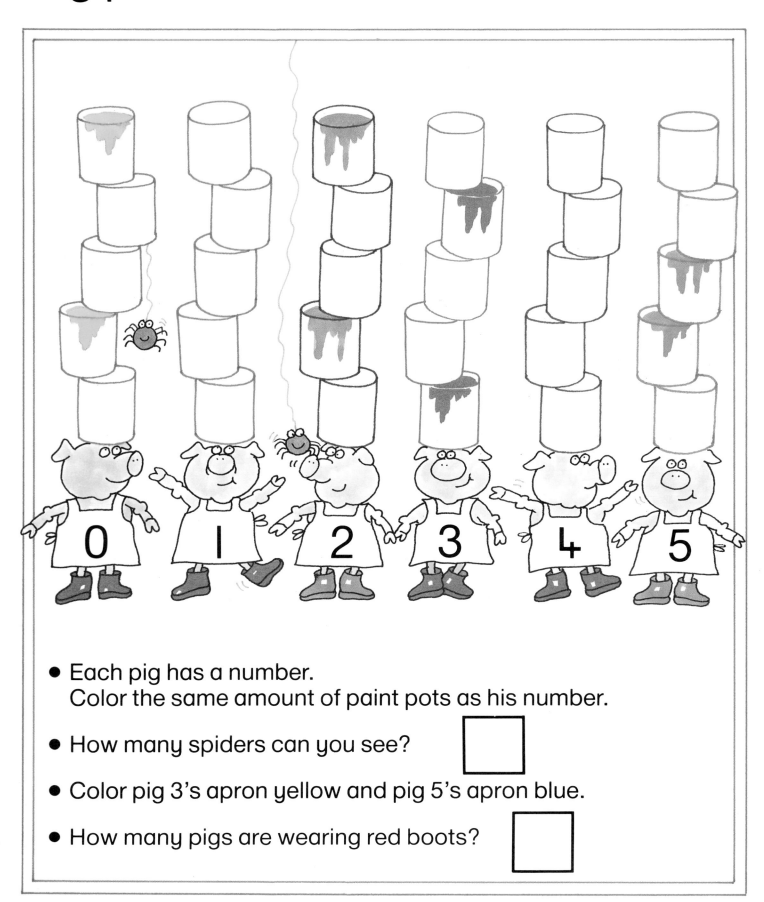

- Each pig has a number.
  Color the same amount of paint pots as his number.

- How many spiders can you see?

- Color pig 3's apron yellow and pig 5's apron blue.

- How many pigs are wearing red boots?

Where are cat, mouse and frog?

● Follow the numbers to find out.

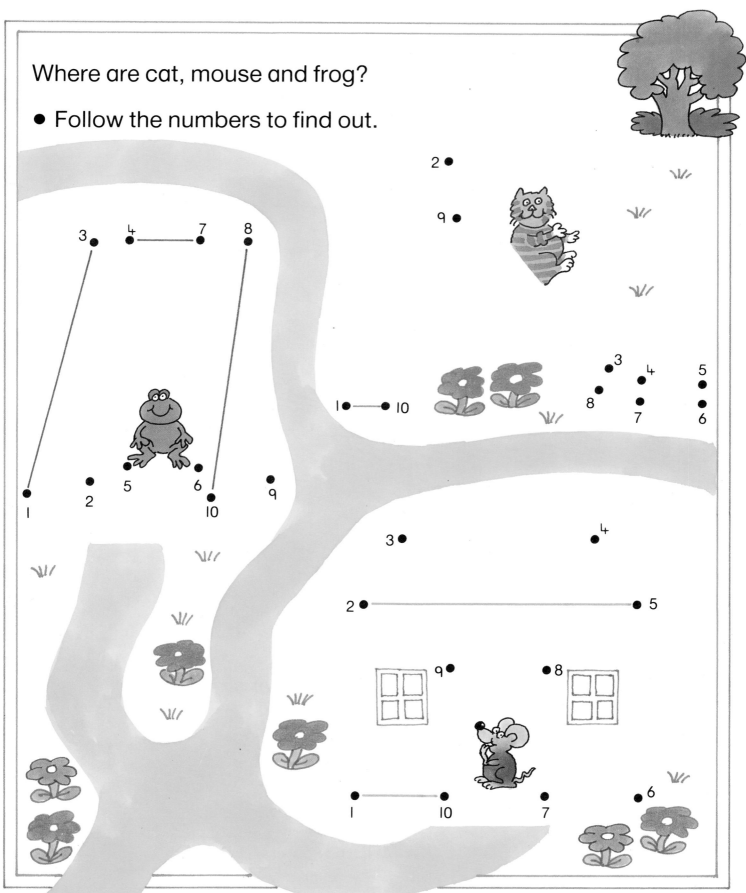

Missing numbers

- The middle shirt on each line has a number. Write the numbers that come before and after it on the other shirts.

- How many spots can you see on the shorts?
  Color the spots red.

- Draw a matching sock on the bottom washing line.

- How many of the shirts are striped?

Same

- How many cats are there? ☐
- How many hats can you see? ☐
- Are there the same number of cats as hats?
- How many mice can you see? ☐
- How many sticks are there? ☐
- Are there the same number of mice as sticks?
- Can you work out which animals are watching the show?

Matching to find more

- Can each frog have a sandwich? Draw lines to find out.

- Circle the correct picture. There are more

- Is there a saucer for each cup? Draw lines to find out.

- Circle the correct picture. There are more

- How many empty plates can you see? Color them in.

Counting to find more

- How many shoes are there? ☐
- How many socks can you find? ☐

- Circle the correct picture. There are more
  Check your answer by drawing lines to join the shoes and socks.

- How many pillows are there? ☐
- How many beds are there? ☐

- Circle the correct picture. There are more

- Which is cat's bed? Which bed belongs to mouse?

Adding on one

- How many crayons can you see? ☐

- Draw 1 more on the table.
  How many crayons are there now? ☐

- How many paint brushes can you see? ☐

- How many do you think there will be
  if you draw one more? ☐

- Draw it in the yellow pot. Are you right?

- How many blocks has frog built into a tower? ☐

- Can you find 5 more blocks to color?

Adding on more than one

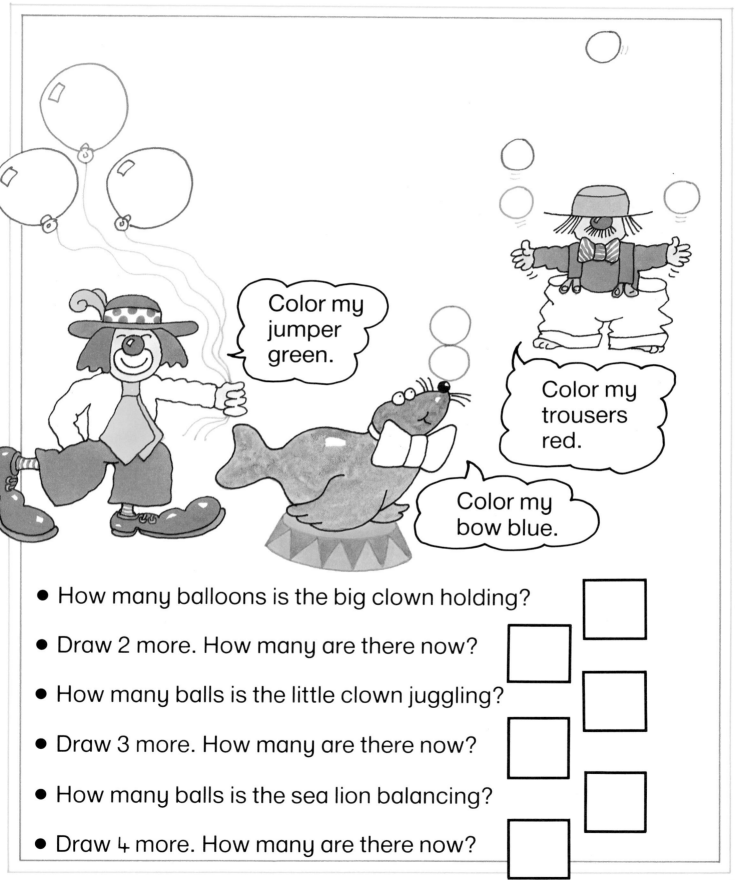

- How many balloons is the big clown holding?

- Draw 2 more. How many are there now?

- How many balls is the little clown juggling?

- Draw 3 more. How many are there now?

- How many balls is the sea lion balancing?

- Draw 4 more. How many are there now?

Cat's toy shop

- Color 3 teddies yellow.
  Color 4 teddies red.
  How many teddies are there altogether?

- Color 6 cars blue.
  Color 2 cars green.
  How many cars are there altogether?

- One kite is patterned. Draw your own pattern on the other.

- What sort of person would wear each of the dressing up hats?

16

Missing buttons

Cat and mouse have lost some buttons from their raincoats.

- How many buttons has cat got?
  He should have 7. Draw in the missing buttons.

- How many have you drawn?

- How many buttons has mouse got?
  He should have 4. Draw in the missing ones.

- How many have you drawn?

Treasure hunt

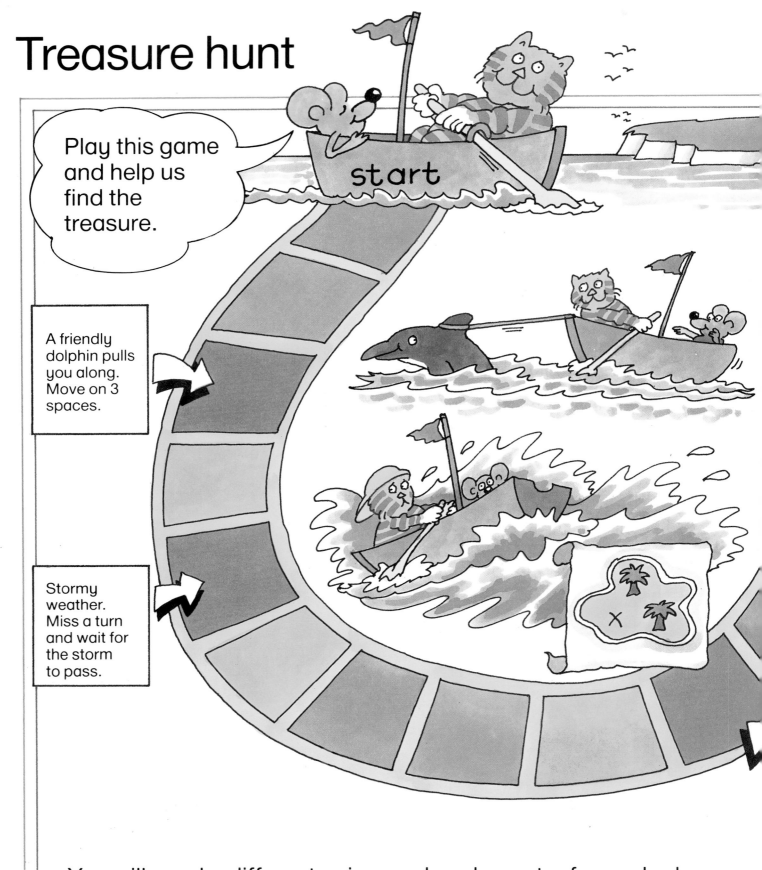

Play this game and help us find the treasure.

A friendly dolphin pulls you along. Move on 3 spaces.

Stormy weather. Miss a turn and wait for the storm to pass.

start

You will need a different coin or colored counter for each player and two dice. Cover 6 on both dice with sticky label. Leave it blank to represent "zero".

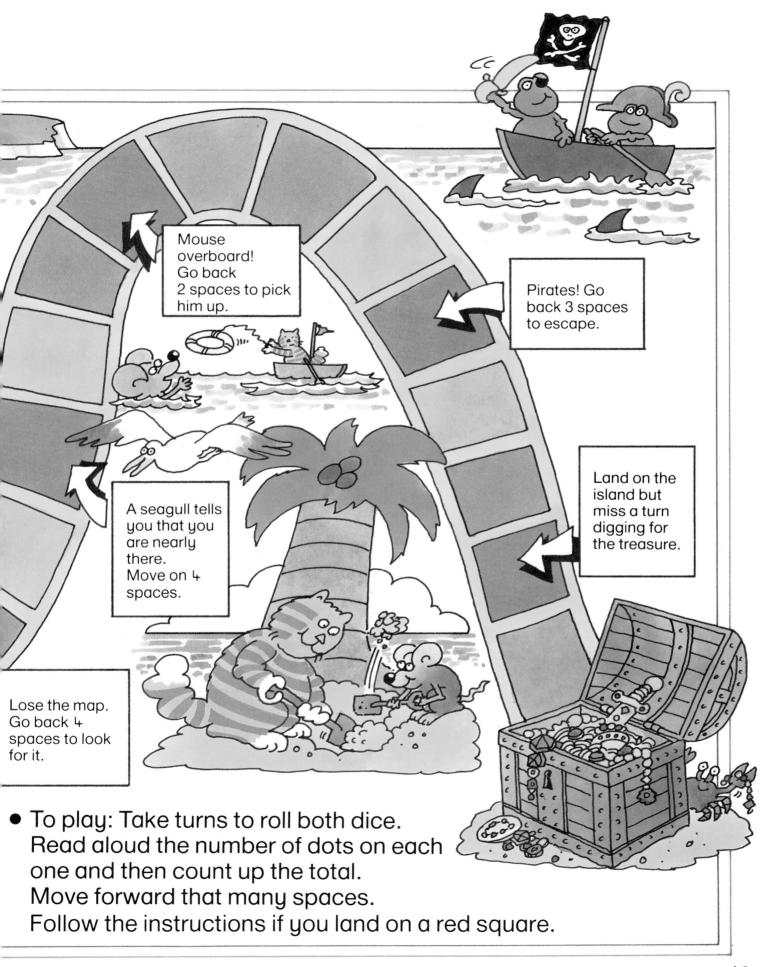

Mouse overboard! Go back 2 spaces to pick him up.

Pirates! Go back 3 spaces to escape.

A seagull tells you that you are nearly there. Move on 4 spaces.

Land on the island but miss a turn digging for the treasure.

Lose the map. Go back 4 spaces to look for it.

- To play: Take turns to roll both dice. Read aloud the number of dots on each one and then count up the total. Move forward that many spaces. Follow the instructions if you land on a red square.

Adding stories

When you want to add numbers together you can use signs instead of words. This is the sign for add:

+

When you have added the numbers together you can use another sign to show you are going to write the answer.

Here is the sign:

=

- Mouse has drawn some signs. Draw circles around the add signs.

- How many racing cars?

☐

- How many birds?

☐

- How many frogs?

☐

20

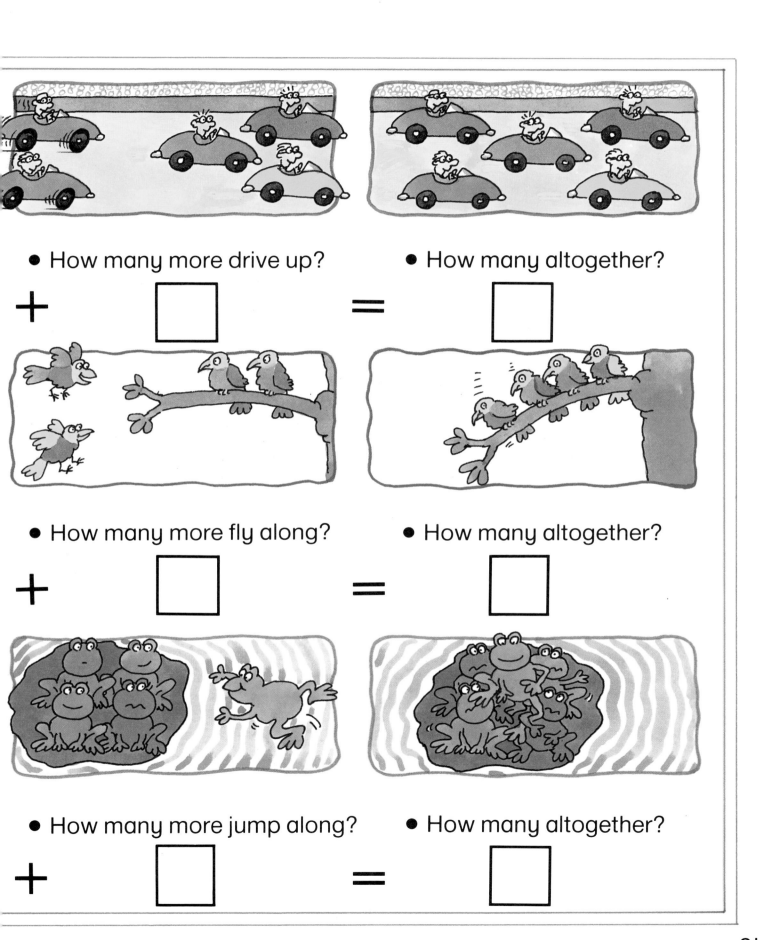

- How many more drive up?

$+$ ☐

- How many altogether?

$=$ ☐

- How many more fly along?

$+$ ☐

- How many altogether?

$=$ ☐

- How many more jump along?

$+$ ☐

- How many altogether?

$=$ ☐

Picture adding

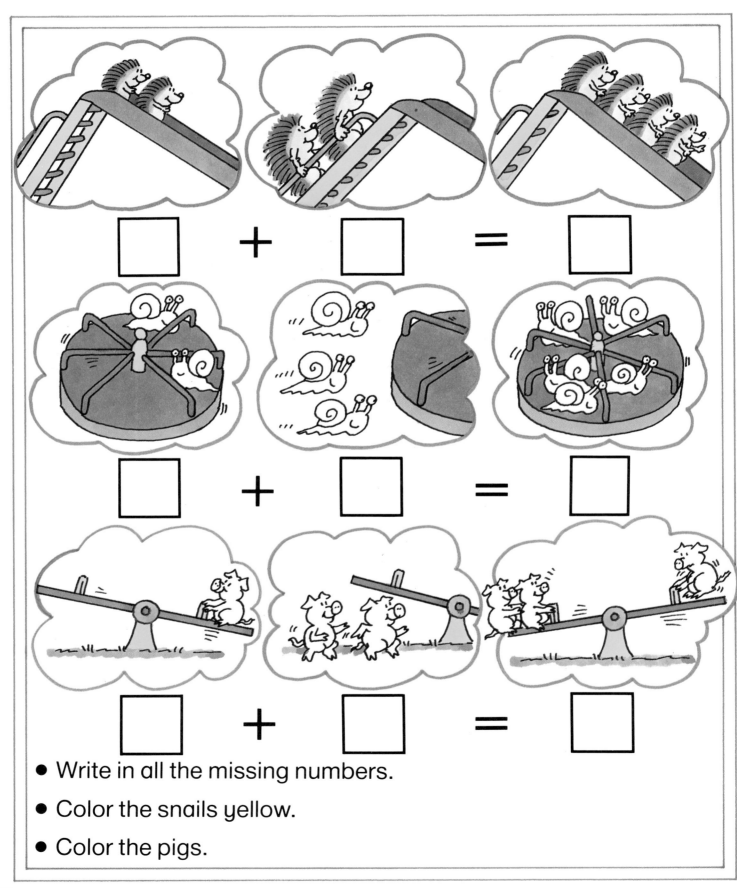

- Write in all the missing numbers.
- Color the snails yellow.
- Color the pigs.

Jigsaw puzzles

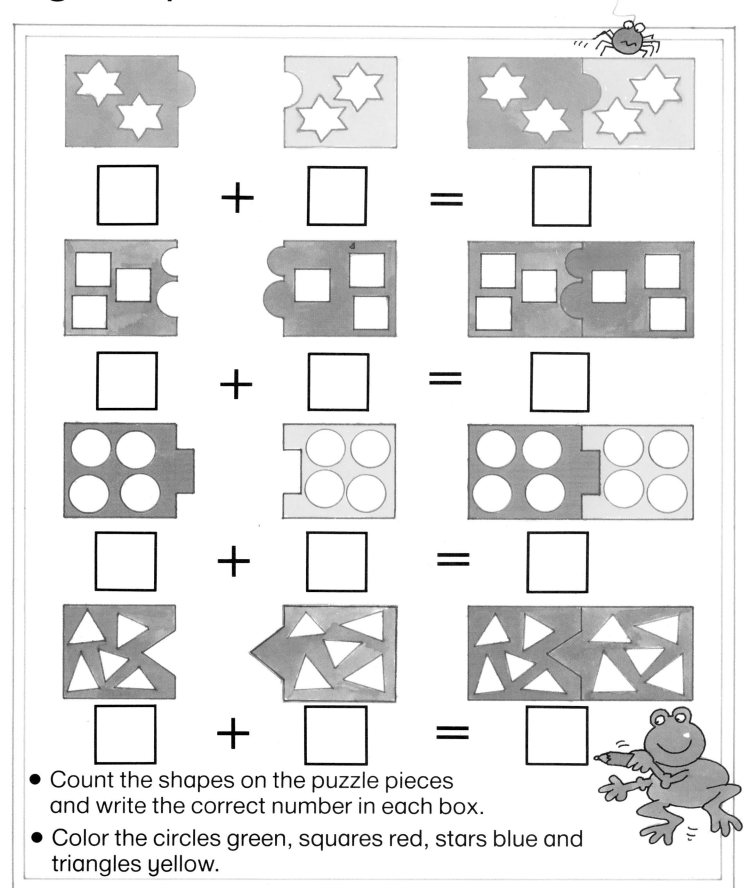

- Count the shapes on the puzzle pieces and write the correct number in each box.
- Color the circles green, squares red, stars blue and triangles yellow.

Animal families

- Write the correct number in each box and find out how many animals are in each family.

- Color in all the baby animals.